DISCARDED

DISCARD

THE SQUIRE TAKES A WIFE

Copyright © 1990 American Teacher Publications
Published by Raintree Publishers Limited Partnership
All rights reserved. No part of this book may be reproduced or utilized in any form or by any
means, electronic or mechanical, including photocopying, recording, or by any information storage
and retrieval system without permission in writing from the Publisher. Inquiries should be
addressed to Raintree Publishers, 310 West Wisconsin Avenue, Milwaukee, Wisconsin 53203.

Library of Congress number: 90-8048

Library of Congress Cataloging in Publication Data

Feldman, Eve.
  The squire takes a wife / by Eve Feldman; illustrated by Bari Weissman.

  (Ready-set-read)
  Summary: A rich squire is determined to marry the farmer's daughter, who is equally determined
that he will not.
  [1. Folklore—Norway.] I. Weissman, Bari, ill. II. Title. III. Series.
PZ8.1.F265Sq 1990   398.22'09481—dc20 [E]   90-8048
ISBN 0-8172-3580-9

1 2 3 4 5 6 7 8 9   94 93 92 91 90

THE SQUIRE TAKES A WIFE

by Eve Feldman
illustrated by Bari Weissman

Raintree Publishers
Milwaukee

Cambridge Central School
Elementary Library

There once was a rich Squire who wanted a wife. One day the Squire saw a girl named Kate.

"That poor farmer's daughter will be happy to marry a rich man like me," thought the Squire. He yelled, "Marry me!"

Kate's father was a poor farmer.
He was afraid to say no, so he gave
his promise.

On Sunday morning the Squire called to his stableboy. "Run to the poor farmer's house. Tell the farmer to send me what he promised."

The boy did what he was told.

"She's in the field," the farmer told the boy. "Go and get her."

The boy did what he was told.

"I've come for what your father
promised the Squire," the boy
told Kate.

"Oh?" said Kate. She had
a merry look in her eye.

12

"Here she is." Kate pointed to the horse. "Take *her* to the Squire."

The boy did what he was told.

13

"Well, sir, I got her and put her in
the stable," said the boy.
"In the stable?" yelled the Squire.
"Take her upstairs!"
"Are you sure, sir?" asked the boy.
"Do what I say! Now!" yelled the Squire.

The boy did what he was told.

"Well, sir, I got her upstairs, but she put up quite a fuss," said the boy.

"Never mind, she'll get used to the idea," said the Squire. "Have the maid dress her in the bridal gown."

"Are you sure, sir?" asked the boy.
"Do what I say! Now!" yelled the Squire.

The boy did what he was told.

"Well, sir, she's dressed, but it wasn't easy!" said the boy.

"Then send her down for the wedding," said the Squire.

"Are you sure, sir?" asked the boy.
"Do what I say! Now!" yelled the Squire.

The boy did what he was told.

When the Squire saw the horse, his face turned red, and he ran out of the hall.

The Squire never did get married . . .

but Kate did!

Cambridge Central School Elementary Library

23

Sharing the Joy of Reading

Reading a book aloud to your child is just one way you can help your child experience the joy of reading. Now that you and your child have shared **The Squire Takes a Wife,** you can help your child begin to think and react as a reader by encouraging him or her to:

• Retell or reread the story with you, looking and listening for the repetition of specific letters, sounds, words, or phrases.

• Make a picture of a favorite character, event, or key concept from this book.

• Talk about his or her own ideas or feelings about the characters in this book and other things that the characters might do.

Here is an activity that you can do together to help extend your child's appreciation of this book: Share another folktale with your child. You can read or retell a folktale found at home or at the library. Maybe your child knows a folktale that he or she would like to retell.